Comet's Big Win

Also by Daisy Sunshine

Twilight, Say Cheese!

Sapphire's Special Power

Shamrock's Seaside Sleepover

UNICORN
University

#4

Comet's
Big Win

★ by DAISY SUNSHINE ★

illustrated by MONIQUE DONG

ALADDIN

New York   London   Toronto   Sydney   New Delhi

❦

ALADDIN

An imprint of Simon & Schuster Children's Publishing Division

1230 Avenue of the Americas, New York, New York 10020

First Aladdin paperback edition October 2021

Text copyright © 2021 by Simon & Schuster, Inc.

Illustrations copyright © 2021 by Monique Dong

Also available in an Aladdin hardcover edition.

All rights reserved, including the right of reproduction in whole or in part in any form.

ALADDIN and related logo are registered trademarks of Simon & Schuster, Inc.

For information about special discounts for bulk purchases, please contact Simon & Schuster Special Sales at 1-866-506-1949 or business@simonandschuster.com.

The Simon & Schuster Speakers Bureau can bring authors to your live event. For more information or to book an event contact the Simon & Schuster Speakers Bureau at 1-866-248-3049 or visit our website at www.simonspeakers.com.

Book designed by Laura Lyn DiSiena

The illustrations for this book were rendered digitally.

The text of this book was set in Tinos.

Manufactured in the United States of America 0921 OFF

2 4 6 8 10 9 7 5 3 1

Library of Congress Cataloging-in-Publication Data

Names: Sunshine, Daisy, author. | Dong, Monique, illustrator.

Title: Comet's big win / by Daisy Sunshine ; illustrated by Monique Dong.

Description: First Aladdin paperback edition. | New York : Aladdin, [2021] | Series: Unicorn University | Summary: At Unicorn University, Comet prefers making kitchen creations in the baking club to playing on the hoofball team, but she tries to do both for the sake of her friendship with Sapphire, however upcoming baking and hoofball competitions may prove to be too much for Comet.

Identifiers: LCCN 2021008698 (print) | LCCN 2021008699 (ebook) |

ISBN 9781534461758 (hardcover) | ISBN 9781534461741 (paperback) | ISBN 9781534461765 (ebook)

Subjects: CYAC: Unicorns—Fiction. | Ability—Fiction. | Clubs—Fiction. | Friendship—Fiction. | Baking—Fiction. | Contests—Ficton. | Boarding schools—Fiction. | Schools—Fiction.

Classification: LCC PZ7.1.S867 Co 2021 (print) | LCC PZ7.1.S867 (ebook) | DDC [Fic]—dc23

LC record available at https://lccn.loc.gov/2021008698

For lovers of sparkles, rainbows, and magic

CONTENTS

Apple-Oat Muffins with Sugar Crystals

Comet couldn't believe her eyes. Unicorn University had been totally transformed!

Today was the school's club fair, and there were tents with waving flags, horns trumpeting joyful music, and cheerful chatter all around her. It looked like a carnival she'd gone to when she was little, but instead of circus performers there were students everywhere. The dance club was performing onstage. The science club was bubbling up purple slime at a booth. There was even a juggling club balancing plates on their horns. All the activity made Comet smile.

Growing up in a large family, Comet had always felt more at home in big, noisy crowds. She felt like she could wander around all day.

Comet soon spotted her three very best friends huddled together over by the gardening club's table. Plants of every color and shape were piled so high, you could hardly see the unicorns in the booth behind them. Shamrock, a mint-colored unicorn with huge, black-rimmed glasses, seemed to be studying a large piece of paper. Twilight, who stood out with her jet-black coat and brightly painted hooves, was looking all around her, clearly distracted by everything that was going on. And Sapphire, a blue unicorn with long braids, was pointing to something on Shamrock's paper with her horn. Comet was sure they were deciding which booth to check out next.

I have to tell them about the baking booth! she remembered. The school's chefs, Stella and Celest, had told her a secret: the first students to get to the baking club booth would get a special treat! And no one made treats like Stella and Celest. The fair was already in full swing, and Comet knew that she and her friends had to get to the baking booth fast. She started running over, but—oh no!—she got a little too excited and her special flying power kicked in. Soon Comet was a rose-colored blur speeding right toward her friends, and with a crash, she knocked them over like bowling pins.

Comet untangled herself from the group while shouting funny apologies. A couple of other unicorns grumbled about the mess, but most unicorns were used to Comet's dramatic entrances. She was still adjusting to her magical ability and was always flying into things or accidently floating away.

Comet and her friends got to their hooves, laughing as the dust settled.

"We were actually just looking for you, Comet," said Twilight.

"Yeah, we were trying to figure out which booth we should check out," Shamrock told her. His glasses had gone crooked in the fall, so he shook his head to straighten them.

"But don't worry, Comet. I already told them you couldn't join any clubs during hoofball season," Sapphire added. She said it matter-of-factly, as if she and Comet had already discussed it.

Comet felt like she had fallen down all over again. *No clubs?!* "What do you mean?" she asked.

"Comet!" Sapphire blew out her lips, giving her friend a look. "Coach told us last week! Everyone on the hoofball team has to be ready for the big game against Glitterhorn College. Which of course means focusing on practice. And nothing else!"

Comet laughed, tossing her bangs out of her eyes. "Oh, come on, Sapphire! We are never going to play in that game. We'll just be there in case, like, *all* the other players get hurt. We're only first years!"

Sapphire shook her head and looked determined. "No way! Coach said we could play if we worked really hard."

Comet just shrugged. They didn't have time to get into this when they really needed to score one of Stella and Celest's surprise treats. "We're wasting time, guys! We have to make it to the baking booth!" Comet broke into a brisk trot before there could be anymore hoofball talk. Sapphire had gotten really into hoofball lately and wanted Comet to be as serious as she was. Comet liked running around on the field with her friends, but she didn't really know why the match against Glitterhorn College was such a big deal.

Sapphire, Shamrock, and Twilight caught up with Comet at the baking booth. She was already munching on an apple-oat muffin sprinkled with crunchy sugar crystals.

"Don't tell anyone, but we saved some muffins for you four!" Stella said, handing them each a sugary treat from a basket stashed under the table. Stella was a dragon with beautiful green scales that sparkled in the afternoon sun.

Celest laughed. "Well, you just said that so loudly, you told everyone yourself!" Celest was a gray speckled unicorn, and the other chef at the school. She and Stella led the baking club every year, in addition to feeding the whole school.

Stella groaned. "Oh, come on. I'm just excited about these award-winning muffins!"

"So, are you guys signing up for the baking club?" Celest asked them. "It's going to be so fun!"

"Sorry, Celest. I've decided on the astronomy club," Shamrock told her. "I was thinking about the science club, but I think I can only do one thing this year."

"Same," Twilight agreed. "I'm going for the art club. Our first project is sculpting! I've never done that before."

"See, Comet?" Sapphire said. "Most unicorns sign up for only one thing. And you already signed up for hoofball."

"Well, I am not your average unicorn!" Comet said. "Where's that baking club sign-up sheet?"

Celest pushed a clipboard her way. "I hope we can handle you, Comet!"

"You probably can't," Comet said, trying to keep a straight face.

Comet looked up from the clipboard to see Sapphire's most serious face staring right at her.

"Comet, this hoofball game is a big deal. Coach is counting on us!" Sapphire told her.

Comet could see how worried her friend was, and was quick to make her feel better. "Really, I can handle both. I'm always sneaking off to the kitchens. This won't be any different!"

Sapphire smiled. "Promise?"

"Super promise with peppermint whipped cream on top," Comet said, giving Sapphire a horn tap.

2

Orange Slices with Cinnamon

The next day, Sapphire and Comet walked toward the field for hoofball practice. The air was crisp and cool, and all the leaves had turned from green to bright oranges, reds, and yellows. Comet watched the swirling leaves whip up and around in the wind, and felt the call of her own hooves wanting to fly up with them. She shook her head and stared at the grass, trying to ground herself. She didn't want to go flying into the whole hoofball team!

"Hey, Comet. Look, here comes Flash," Sapphire pointed out.

Flash was the captain of the hoofball team, and Comet and Sapphire agreed that she was the coolest unicorn at Unicorn University. She tied back her rainbow mane with a purple bandanna and always wore sparkly blue eyeliner, even to practice. Plus, she was the best player on the team. Flash could pull off this awesome spin-and-kick move that no one else would even try. Everyone on the team looked up to her.

"Hey, Saph! Com!" Flash greeted them. She had a bag of hoofballs slung around her neck. "Ready for practice?"

"Totally!" Sapphire squeaked. "We can't wait to win against Glitterhorn!"

"Awesome!" Flash cheered. "Hey, I'd better get going. I told Coach I'd help her set up for practice. See you guys soon!"

Flash broke into a gallop and ran up ahead of them. She was also the fastest unicorn in the school, so it wasn't long before she was out of sight.

"Can you believe it?" Sapphire asked.

"Flash totally talked to us! And she gave us *nicknames*," Comet said.

Sapphire and Comet chatted about their good luck all the way to the field, and stopped only when Coach's sharp whistle blew to gather the team together before practice.

Comet smelled the grass and dirt that got kicked up as the team huddled together, and she smiled as the cool breeze brushed the side of her cheek.

"Okay, team!" Coach boomed so that everyone could hear. "As you all know, the big game is just two weeks away, and we need to get ready. Today we're going to focus on our magical strategies. So, who can remind everyone of the rules about magical abilities?"

"You can use your magic for only thirty seconds at a time, so make sure to have a plan," Flash said.

"Can you give us an example?" Coach asked.

"Well, I can change my appearance, you know? Sometimes

it helps for me to distract the other team by flashing different colors. Just to get a little advantage. You have to work with what you've got."

"Precisely. Let's break into twos. Think about how your abilities could help you in the game," Coach told them.

The team broke up into pairs and spread out over the field.

As usual, Comet and Sapphire found their favorite spot by the bleachers.

"You know, you have the best ability for hoofball, Comet," Sapphire said.

Comet laughed. "No way! Remember yesterday when I knocked everyone over? What would happen if I did that during a game?"

"If you knocked over the *other* team, it would be great!" Sapphire smiled. "I mean it, though. Like, what if I kicked the ball up to you? You can totally control your floating now."

Comet thought about it. She *had* gotten better at floating above the ground. Just as long as she didn't fly up too high and didn't move too much. Sapphire usually had good ideas, so Comet always trusted her vision. And Sapphire had a great kick. She could always make the hoofball do exactly what she wanted. "Okay, let's try it!" Comet ran down the field a little and hovered above the ground. "Go for it!"

Sapphire kicked the ball into the air so that it went right by Comet's front left hoof. Comet got to it just in time and sent it soaring across the field all the way to the goal!

"Comet! You scored!" Sapphire cheered.

"No, *we* scored!" Comet called back.

The two friends jumped up and down, cheering "We scored! We scored!" until Coach told them to settle down and get focused on practice.

After running some other drills, Coach blew the whistle to signal the end of practice.

Time for my favorite part! Comet thought as she saw Flash carrying a tray filled with orange slices sprinkled with cinnamon. Comet zoned out as her mind drifted to thoughts of baking. *Maybe I'll try to make an orange-and-cinnamon cake, or even ice cream! I'll have to ask Stella if—*

"Comet, listen!" Sapphire hissed. Comet looked up to see Coach speaking to the team about extra hoofball practices.

"Oops, sorry!" Comet whispered.

3

Breakfast Biscuits

The next morning, Comet work up early. She was meeting the baking club so they could make a breakfast feast together before classes started. Comet couldn't think of a better way to start the day.

The stables were still cold in the early morning air, so she pulled her cozy blanket around her shoulders and left her stall. The snores and sighs of her classmates surrounded her as she crept quietly outside.

Even the sun was still waking up, peeking over the rolling hills and filling the sky with bright orange-and-pink light. Comet's breath created little clouds as she made her way to the kitchens.

Soon she could see friendly smoke blooming from the crooked stone chimney, and the glow of a cozy fire through the big kitchen window. Comet trotted the rest of the way, eager to get started.

A few other unicorns arrived at the kitchens just as Comet did.

"Hey, Storm!" Comet called to her classmate, a three-legged gray unicorn.

"Mornin'," Storm mumbled as she shuffled toward the door. She looked half-asleep.

Stella ushered everyone into the kitchen. The big wooden table had five baking stations set up. Each place had a mixing bowl, two eggs, a measuring cup filled with flour, a glass of milk, a stick of butter, and a kitchen towel. And a horn-written recipe next to each place.

Comet took her spot by two unicorns with matching

gold heart charms hanging from their necks.

"Hi, I'm Glinda! And this is Spark," the unicorn closest to her said, her charm wiggling as she pointed to the bright purple unicorn beside her.

"Hey. I'm Comet! I just love your charms."

"They're friendship charms!" Spark told her.

Comet was about to ask her more about them, but Stella was starting class. "Good morning! Take your places, everyone!" she said, gesturing with her long, flour-covered claws.

"Today we're making biscuits. Let's start by studying the recipe," Celest added. She and Stella wore matching white aprons, not that the fabric had done much to keep them free of flour dust. Stella had a streak of flour over her eye, and Celest's usually glittering horn was totally covered.

The class got to work reading their recipe cards. Once everyone had looked over the measurements and instructions, the kitchen soon filled with laughter and the comforting sounds of bowls clanging together. Comet had made

biscuits lots of times, but they'd always turned out a little dry. Not like the fluffy ones Stella and Celest made. She was excited to learn their secret.

It wasn't long before Comet was in the baking zone. The smells of the kitchen always grounded her. Her hooves weren't trying to fly away, because they were right where they wanted to be. When she spotted the bowl of oranges on the counter, Comet had an idea. She crept over to the counter and grabbed a few from the bowl, along with another special ingredient. Her biscuits were going to be *awesome*. Or at least she hoped!

Comet could feel her heart flutter as she pushed her tray of biscuits into the oven. She tried to keep the smile off her face as, through the oven window, she watched the dough rise. She had a feeling these would wow the club.

Soon everyone's biscuits were pulled from the oven and the club members displayed their fluffy creations on the big wooden table. Everyone went around and tasted what each unicorn had made. Comet wasn't the only one who'd added a special twist.

Stormy laughed when Spark asked her why she'd added candy to her breakfast. "Because chocolate makes everything better!"

Glinda blew out her cheeks as she looked at her own biscuits. They had all somehow melted down into a sludge that covered the baking sheet. "Even chocolate couldn't have saved these," she groaned.

"Wow, Comet! These are the best biscuits I've ever had," said Stormy after wandering over to Comet's station. "Where did you get the idea for the orange-and-cinnamon flavor?"

"Hoofball!" Comet cheered. Stormy just raised her eyebrows.

"Okay, bakers!" Stella called, quieting the club. "It's time for you to get to class. See you next week, same time and place!"

Comet had study hall in the library as her first class of the day, so she hung back to help with cleanup. It looked like a sugary explosion in the kitchen.

"You know, your biscuits really were spectacular, Comet," Stella said as they wiped down the table.

Comet blushed. "I just added a little extra spice. I saw it on the counter and felt like it would be the perfect thing!"

"A true baker!" Celest said. "You listened to the ingredients. You know, you should enter the baking competition against Glitterhorn in a couple of weeks. It's right after the hoofball match."

"That's true!" Stella

agreed. "You're always surprising me with your baking, Comet."

"It's not as big a deal as the hoofball match, of course," Celest added quickly.

Stella laughed. "Only the baking club shows up at the tent to watch. I guess baking is not quite as exciting as hoofball."

Comet didn't agree. She loved reading cookbooks, and being in the kitchen was just as fun as being on the hoofball field. And even though she could hear Sapphire's objections already, she couldn't help but be interested in the idea of baking in the competition.

"If you win, you get to compete in the Five Kingdoms Bakeoff, against kids from all over the world! Which is better than a trophy, I think," Celest said.

"And you get to bring friends. Every baker goes with a team of three others. I have a feeling I know some unicorns who would like to travel to the competition with you. It's in a new place every year," Stella added.

"We could set up some extra lessons to help you get ready! That would be fun. I really think you could be our best shot at winning. Truth be told, we usually lose," Celest said.

"Wow, I would love to," Comet told them, feeling her cheeks heat up. No one had ever said she was the best before. Maybe the silliest. But never the best. She felt as warm as her freshly baked biscuits.

4

The Secret Ingredient

Comet was so excited, she half walked, half floated out of the kitchens. She wondered what a baking competition would be like. Comet had always loved baking for her friends and for her family, but no one had ever taken her passion so seriously before. It was an amazing feeling.

As she made her way across the lawn, she was surprised to see Sapphire, practically floating herself.

Uh-oh. Comet suddenly felt flatter than a pancake. *What will she think of the baking competition?*

"Comet!" Sapphire yelled, running over when she saw

her friend. "You won't believe what happened! Coach told me the best news."

Comet smiled at Sapphire's good mood. Maybe this would all work out! "No way! Because I just got glitter-tastic news too!"

"Me first," Sapphire said. "Coach and Flash saw our move yesterday, the one where I kick and you float? And they want us to do it in the game. Coach called us the secret ingredient. I'm so excited. They're going to add extra practices just for us!" The words rushed out of her, like she couldn't tell her friend fast enough.

Comet couldn't help but smile, seeing Sapphire so excited. "Wow, Sapphire!"

"Baking club won't mess with practices, right?" Sapphire asked. "Remember you promised!"

Comet's heart skipped a beat. How could she tell Sapphire about the baking competition now? She didn't want to break a promise.

"I mean, you don't really need me for the special move," Comet told her, biting her bottom lip. "It's all about your perfect kick!"

Sapphire smiled. "No way! We're a team! I totally need you."

Comet didn't know what to say. She didn't want to let Sapphire down. Maybe she could do both things? *The competition is after the hoofball match*, she thought. *I can totally pull this off! Easy peasy.* Comet puffed herself up like a soufflé fresh out of the oven.

"Actually, you're right! This is great!" Comet told her. "Does this mean we get to hang out with Flash?"

She thought about telling Sapphire that she was also going to enter the baking competition, but she couldn't quite get the words out before Sapphire said, "Yes! And it's super rare for first years to play in the Glitterhorn game. Our name could be on a trophy!"

Comet laughed as Sapphire sang, "We're going to get a trophy! We're going to get a trophy!" all the way to their first classes of the day.

But Comet couldn't quite shake the feeling that she had done something wrong. *Should I have told her about the baking contest?* she thought as she trailed behind Sapphire. *Oh, but she would just worry. And that would distract her from the big game!* After quite a bit of back-and-forth with

herself, Comet decided that the best thing was to keep the baking competition a secret. Then no one would worry and everyone would be happily surprised when she won! Really, what could go wrong?

5

A Cup of Tea and a Cookie

The next week flew by. Comet had been so busy with all the extra practices that she could hardly believe the Glitterhorn competitions were now only a week away.

"You know, Comet, I think I'm going to start calling you 'the Blur,'" Twilight said as Comet grabbed an apple from their lunch tree.

"What do you mean?" Comet asked with her mouth full. She had time for only a quick break before rushing off to baking practice, but she had promised Twilight they would have lunch together. Comet was starting to think she should stop making promises altogether.

"You're always running from one place to the next," Twilight told her. "I never see you anymore. Is everything okay?"

Comet rolled her eyes. "Of course! Just, you know, busy."

"Okay—" Twilight started, but Comet didn't let her finish.

"I'm sorry, but I gotta go!" Comet said, partly so she wouldn't be late and partly because she knew that if they kept talking, she would let her big secret slip. Comet had stuck to her plan, and only the baking club knew she was training for the baking competition. Comet told herself she was keeping a secret because she didn't want anyone to worry about her, but when she looked back at Twilight's crestfallen face, she wondered if she was doing the right thing.

After a brisk gallop, Comet pushed open the big wooden door to the kitchen, and stifled her yawn when she saw Stella coming toward her with an apron. Comet didn't want her to know how tired she was. Stella and Celest were helping her so much, and on top of their job of feeding the school! She didn't want to let them down.

"Good afternoon, Comet," Celest said from across the room. She peered over her wire-rimmed reading glasses. A gigantic cookbook was open in front of her.

Comet smiled when she saw all the little handwritten notes in the margins and the food splotches that stained the old pages. There was something about old cookbooks that Comet had always loved. They made her feel like she was connected to generations of bakers.

"What's that for?" she asked, pointing to the cookbook with her horn.

"To help you find your special cake recipe, of course," Stella said.

Comet blinked, confused for a moment. "Oh! The one I'll bake at the competition?"

"Have you thought of any ideas, dear?" Celest added,

clearly trying to hide the concern in her voice. "We have only a week to prepare, after all."

Comet blushed, her already pink cheeks turning a deep shade of red. "Um—I meant to last night before bed but, well, I fell asleep." She felt like she'd burned their batch of chocolate chip cookies. The truth was that she had lain awake thinking about possible recipes, but nothing seemed good enough. The whole baking club was so excited for her. What if she wasn't as good a baker as they thought?

"Why don't you look through this book now? We can take a break from practicing, and I'll make you a cup of tea," Celest told her kindly.

Comet felt her whole body relax at the idea. A quiet minute alone with a cookbook? She almost cried with relief. "Thank you so much."

When she was all settled by the book with her cup of tea and a cinnamon sugar cookie, she began to study recipes from all over the five kingdoms. She couldn't believe

how many different types of cakes there were. Some sounded amazing, like the triple chocolate cake with chocolate whipped cream, and some sounded not so good, like prune cake with candied twigs. She searched for one to make for the competition. She had to choose a cake that best represented her school. Which seemed impossible. There were so many different parts of Unicorn University! How could one cake represent everyone? And, the worst thought of all, what if it turned out wrong?

Comet tried to shake her doubts off and kept turning the weathered pages. There was still plenty of time to figure it out. Right?

6

A Lump of Uncooked Dough

C omet? Comet! Wake up!"

"Huh? Where am I?" Comet whipped her head around and accidently knocked over a stack of books. The pile of cookbooks she had meant to look through all tumbled to the floor, making the whole library turn and say, "Shush!"

"You're in a library, not a barn!" a unicorn at the table next to them said. Comet could only see a sparkling horn above that unicorn's own stack of books.

"Sorry," Comet whispered. She glanced at Shamrock.

His bushy eyebrows were furrowed over his glasses. He seemed worried. "Comet, are you okay?"

Comet felt her jaw set. She was so sick of people asking her that. She'd been practicing for the baking competition and the hoofball match for the past two weeks, and, sure, she was tired. But she was more tired of Shamrock and Twilight giving her sad looks and asking how she was all the time. The competitions with Glitterhorn were the next day. Couldn't everyone leave her alone until everything was all over?

"ARGH! Shamrock, if you ask me that one more time, I swear I'm going to . . . I'm going to . . ." Comet huffed. "I will be super mad at you!"

Shamrock frowned. "It's just that you keep falling asleep. I mean, we were in the middle of a conversation, and then—poof!—you nodded off. Again."

Comet sighed. That *was* pretty rude of her. "I'm sorry. I only have to get through tomorrow, and then I'll be back to normal."

"Is it all the extra hoofball practice?"

"And all the baking—" Comet stopped short, because just then a couple of older unicorns from the hoofball team stopped by the table and said cheery hellos to her.

"Can't wait to get that trophy tomorrow," said Blaze, a bright orange unicorn with a neon-yellow mane.

"You and Sapphire are sure going to give Glitterhorn a

big surprise!" a silver unicorn named Star squealed.

"Totally," Comet said, wondering if she believed it.

Comet groaned as they walked away. *That was close,* she thought. She had been keeping the baking competition to herself. She didn't want the team to find out and think she wasn't taking the secret ingredient plan seriously. Everyone on the team was so excited about her and Sapphire's secret move, and Comet had never felt so popular. It would have been nice, if she hadn't felt terrified that she was going to let them all down.

Shamrock waited until the hoofball group was out of earshot. "Baking?" he asked quietly. "I thought the baking club only met once a week."

"Yeah, you know," Comet said, thinking quickly, "and all the—uh—stress baking."

Shamrock nodded. "We have noticed how stressed you've been—"

"You've been talking about me behind my horn?"

"We've only been saying that we're worried about you!"

Comet felt like she had swallowed a lump of uncooked dough. "Shamrock, you don't know anything about this. Or hoofball!" She stomped on the floor with frustration.

The unicorn peeked over their stack of books to hiss, "I'm going to tell Professor Jazz on you!"

"Don't worry, I'm leaving!" Comet told them as she gathered the cookbooks from the floor. It felt like a kettle was whistling inside her. She wondered if smoke was coming out of her ears.

Shamrock's eyebrows disappeared behind his glasses frames as his face fell into a deep frown. "I'm sorry, Comet. I was only trying to help."

"Well, don't!"

Comet left the library with tears in her eyes. Shamrock didn't understand. She could totally handle it. She would show him.

7

Apple-Cider Doughnuts

Comet huffed and puffed past groups of students on the main lawn, where they were hanging out on blankets and eating snacks. *Must be nice.*

Comet was hustling toward her last practice with Sapphire and Flash. A couple of weeks earlier she would have been so excited to hang out with her best friend and the coolest unicorn in school. But hoofball was so not fun anymore. They just did the same thing over and over. And somehow it felt like Comet was getting worse. She could tell Sapphire was getting more and more disappointed in her. With a sigh, Comet dragged herself toward the practice field. *At least it's the last practice. Tomorrow I'll either make it work . . . or I won't.*

She made her way along a forest path, fallen leaves crunching beneath her hooves and the wind whistling through the trees. There was something about this weather that always made her want to make apple-cider doughnuts with fresh cider. Comet smiled, thinking she would ask Stella and Celest if they could make some tomorrow morning. *Maybe that would be a good idea for the competition cake,* she thought. She couldn't believe she hadn't thought of a cake yet. How could the next day be the last lesson before the competition? Comet had told Stella and Celest that she had already figured out a recipe and was just keeping it a surprise. It felt like she was lying to everyone, and she didn't know how much more of all this she could take. *It'll be over tomorrow,* she reminded herself.

"Comet! Over here!"

Comet looked up to see Twilight standing by a tree with her easel and paints all set up. Comet trotted over, wanting to see what her friend was creating.

The scene was of the forest, but the leaves were still green. There was a bright blue sky with a brilliant rainbow over the trees. She'd even included the top of the library's crystal towers and the red stables in the distance. The scene looked just like it had on Comet's first day of school.

"Wow, Twilight. I love all the colors you've used. It's beautiful."

"Thanks, Comet. I've been working on it for ages." Twilight laughed softly. "The leaves were still green when I started!"

"But what about sculpting with the art club?"

Twilight shrugged. "I'm terrible at it, but it's fun to hang out with other artists. It's just, sometimes I need to have some time alone, you know? This painting makes me feel calm. Like I'm exactly where I'm supposed to be when I

have a paintbrush." Twilight blushed. "Maybe that doesn't make any sense."

"No, it does! Baking is like that for me. Or it used to be at least."

"Used to be?"

Comet sighed. She looked at Twilight for a long time before deciding she couldn't keep it to herself any longer. "Can you keep a secret?"

"Um, I think so."

That was good enough for Comet. "I entered a baking competition against Glitterhorn. It's right after the hoofball match tomorrow. Stella and Celest have been giving me extra lessons." She looked at Twilight out of the corner of her eye, worried about what she would say.

"You're the best baker I know! You'll win for sure."

Comet smiled. "Well . . . if I do win, I get to compete in another round against kids from all over the five kingdoms.

I can even bring three friends with me."

Twilight's eyes sparkled. "That would be amazing. And, you know, Sapphire has always wanted to travel. She would love to hear about this."

Comet shook her head. "No way. I think she cares more about hoofball right now than anything else. And she is already annoyed with me."

"But you've been practicing for hoofball every day!"

"And baking every morning before school, but I'm worried I'm getting worse at both. Yesterday I accidently made an explosion by mixing baking powder with some wrong ingredients. Then later at hoofball practice, I couldn't even get my hoof to hit the ball!" Comet took a breath. She had been trying so hard to bottle all these feelings up, and now they were bursting out. *Kinda like my baking fail yesterday*, she thought. "I feel like I'm lying to everyone. Especially Sapphire. What would she say?"

Twilight paused to think. She always chose her words

wisely. Comet admired that about her. For Comet, words tumbled out of her mouth like apples from a ripped bag.

"She knows how much you love baking," Twilight finally said. "And I think she would love the chance to travel somewhere. She might not be completely happy at first, but I think she'd understand and be excited in the end."

Comet considered this as she stared at Twilight's beautiful painting. It *was* calming. Feeling a little better, Comet thought, *Twilight's right. How could Sapphire be mad if I won the hoofball match and the baking prize?* She just had to win. Then she could tell Sapphire everything. "You're right. I can't let her down. Not in the hoofball game. And not with the baking prize."

"Comet, I didn't mean—"

But the final class bell interrupted her and reminded Comet where she was supposed to be.

"Oh no! I'm going to be late for practice. Thanks for talking with me, Twilight. This really helped. I just need to focus and do this. For Sapphire! For Unicorn University!"

"That's not really what I meant. . . ."

But Comet was already a rose-colored blur shooting toward the fields.

Comet skidded to a stop in front of Flash and Sapphire, accidently splattering them with mud. *Oops.*

"Hey, Comet," Flash said, looking at her mud-specked flanks. "Let me go get some towels."

"Comet!" Sapphire groaned as Flash walked away. "You're late again! I can't believe—"

"I know, I know," Comet said, trying to cut Sapphire off before things got too heated. "But I ran into Twilight and we had a really good talk, and—"

"I just don't know where your horn's at, Comet! You are always late to practice. And then when you're here, you don't pay attention and—"

"Listen! I know I haven't been great, but I promise I'm here for you—"

"No, you listen!" Sapphire was shouting now. "I know you can be silly, but our move is my only chance to get into this game. And I really want to play! If I could fly and kick, I would. But I'm counting on you, Comet."

Comet froze. She didn't know what to say and could feel tears welling up. Not wanting Sapphire to see her cry, she ran down the field to get into position. "Okay, let's get started!" she yelled, her voice wavering just a little.

Sapphire scraped the ground with her hooves. "Comet! I'm—"

"Okay, let's go!" Flash blew a whistle. "We're running out of sunshine here."

Comet and Sapphire ran their special play over and over, but Comet kept messing up. First she couldn't even make herself float, which sometimes happened when she was feeling low. Then when she could float, she was all wobbly and couldn't kick the ball.

After what felt like the millionth try, Sapphire ran over to Comet.

"Hey, Comet, is this because of what I said? I'm really sorry. Sometimes my competitive side gets the best of me. You're doing great, I promise."

"Okay, you two!" Flash yelled from across the field. "Final goal before the Glitterhorn game!" She kicked the ball toward the goal, but it veered close to Sapphire and Comet. Sapphire leapt up and kicked the ball toward the goal. Score!

"Wow, Sapphire," said Comet. "I don't think you guys need me. Maybe tomorrow—"

But Sapphire interrupted her. "I do need you, Comet! We're partners. I'm sorry I wasn't fair before."

Flash ran over to them before Comet could say anything else. "Don't worry, Comet. I think it's just nerves. You'll do better tomorrow," Flash told her. "Let's go get some dinner."

8

Biscuits and Candied Apples

It was Saturday morning, and the whole school was getting ready for Glitterhorn's arrival. Comet walked through the main lawn as students hung up a welcome banner and set up tents. The Sparklers, the school band, tuned their instruments onstage as the dancing club warmed up for their routine. The whole school felt alive, and everyone seemed so excited.

For the first time in her life, Comet felt like she wanted to run away from the crowd. She wished she could go back to her stable and hide in her stall all day. In her team uniform—a short cape with the letters *UU* stitched onto the back—she looked the part of a hoofball player, but she felt like a fraud.

Comet forced herself to walk to the school kitchen for one more morning lesson. She had no idea how she would admit that she didn't have a plan for the competition cake. It was just that every time she thought about it, she would get a wave of nerves and would start to worry about disappointing people. So she had kept putting it off. And now she was out of time.

The sight of the chimney smoke did make her smile, if only a little. It always made her feel at home. Comet pushed open the big wooden door and was met with a surprise.

Shamrock, Twilight, Stella, and Celest were all gathered around the table. There were apple-oat muffins, biscuits, and candied apples piled high in front of them.

"You're finally here!" Celest cheered.

"We came to surprise you!" Twilight said. "I told

Shamrock what's been going on. I'm sorry I didn't keep your secret, Comet. But I figured you needed all the support you could get." Twilight shimmered a little, becoming invisible and then visible again. Like Comet, Twilight found that her ability to control her special power could be swayed by her emotions.

"Thank you for telling him, Twilight," Comet told her honestly. "I wish I had told you both earlier. You could've helped!"

Comet had tears in her eyes. She was overwhelmed by all the love in this little room. She gave Shamrock a hug, hanging her head over his neck and squeezing him tight. "I'm sorry I've been so rude!"

Shamrock just shook his head. "Don't even worry about it."

"And look! The doughnuts are ready!" Stella turned toward her from the oven, carrying a tray of freshly baked treats.

Everyone dug into the food, and Comet was grateful no one mentioned any kind of competition. As she looked around the table of treats, Comet was suddenly struck with an idea. "I know what I'm going to bake today!" she shouted to the room.

Stella and Celest looked at each other with raised eyebrows. Comet realized they'd known all along that she hadn't had a plan. She couldn't help but laugh.

"Twilight, do you think you can coordinate with the sculpting club before the baking contest?" Comet asked.

"We have a booth set up and we're giving demonstrations. What do you need?"

Comet filled them in on her plans. Everyone was on board.

"Now I think it's time you get to that hoofball match," Celest reminded her with a wink when everything was settled.

"We'll bring all the supplies!" Stella boomed as Comet dashed out the door.

Comet left the kitchen feeling better than she had in weeks. She even managed to fly the whole way without running into anything!

9

The Real Secret Ingredient

The field didn't look like the stretch of grass and goals Comet had come to know. The simple wooden goals had been shined and polished so that they sparkled in the morning light, and a brand-new net hung between the posts. The grass was freshly cut, and freshly painted wooden stands had been put up so that more unicorns could watch the game.

The Glitterhorn team practiced on one side of the field. True to their name, each player had a special glittering sleeve over their horn with a sparkling letter *G*. Comet was suddenly worried. They seemed so much more serious than Unicorn U.

"Comet! Comet!" Coach waved her over to the team huddle.

"I have a little surprise for the team," Flash was saying as Comet joined the circle. Using her horn, Flash opened a bag. Inside were tons of purple bandannas, just like Flash's! "I thought we could all wear them for the game!"

The team cheered and helped each other loop the bright fabric around horns and tie back manes. Everyone had a different style, but they still looked like a team. Comet stood just outside the huddle, looping her bandanna around her ankle. She thought the team looked super cool, and everyone looked so happy. But she couldn't help feeling like she was an outsider looking in. She tried to shake off the feeling and get her head in the game.

Soon the referee blew the whistle to signal it was time to play, and everyone took their places. Comet and Sapphire waited on the sidelines together. Usually they would be whispering and giggling as they watched, but neither of them said anything. Comet felt like the air was buzzing with all the things she wanted to admit to her friend.

Flash bedazzled the other team by turning her mane from pink to purple to teal and got the ball from the first ball toss. Before the other team knew what was happening, she ran the ball down the field and scored! The crowd went wild, but Comet couldn't stop looking at the clock. If the game went into overtime, she'd miss the start of the baking competition. She floated up just a little to see the tops of the baking tent, and wondered what was going on inside it.

The other team was back on their hooves fast, working together to pass the ball to each other so quickly that the Unicorn U players could barely keep track. Glitterhorn swept past all the lines of defense and scored.

Coach called Sapphire and Comet over.

"Time to add our secret ingredient!" Flash told them

with a wink. "You guys can do this! Don't worry about yesterday."

Comet felt like her hooves were stuck in the mud, as if her whole body were telling her not to go. She looked over to Sapphire and saw that her friend was feeling totally different. It looked like Sapphire was shining from the inside out as she did a little excited prance along the sidelines.

"This is our moment! I want to remember this feeling forever," Sapphire cheered.

Comet never wanted to feel this way again. *I wish I could feel like Sapphire, but it feels like my heart is split in two*, she thought. And just like that, Comet knew what she had to do. She hoped everyone would understand.

"Actually, Coach," Comet said, her voice wavering a little. She could feel the whole team's eyes on her. "Sapphire is your secret ingredient, not me."

Coach looked away from the field to stare at Comet. "What do you mean?"

"Yeah, Comet, what do you mean?" Sapphire looked totally confused. Everyone did.

Comet could hear the cheers from the unicorns on the sidelines and knew she was making the right decision. She took a deep breath.

"Your secret weapon is Sapphire's perfect kick. All I do is float. And honestly, I'd probably mess up. My heart isn't on the field today. It's in the baking tent. I've been trying to

live up to your expectations, Sapphire, instead of listening to my heart. And it's taken me away from what I really love."

Sapphire looked stunned. "Huh? What baking tent?"

"You don't need me, Sapphire," Comet told her. "You have the best kick on the whole team, and you can jump higher than anyone else. Have Flash kick it to you a little high, and jump and kick like yesterday. I know you guys can do it. Way better than I ever could. This is *your* moment, Sapphire."

Sapphire just shook her head with surprise.

Comet turned away from her teammates. She didn't want to see their faces as she dashed away from the field. She knew she had made the right decision. She hoped they would see it too.

10

The Last-Minute Cake

Comet could see the baking tent. It was made of billowing white fabric, with flags perched atop three points of the tent. They waved merrily in the distance. Comet dashed toward them, finally ready for her own moment to shine.

Inside the tent, the baking club surrounded the Unicorn University table, with Twilight and Shamrock.

A golden unicorn stood at the other table. Like the Glitterhorn hoofball team, he was wearing a glittering horn cover with a sparkling *G* in the center. Comet looked down at the purple bandanna tied around her ankle and tried not to think about what her team must have been feeling right then.

An older unicorn with wire-rimmed glasses and a pink beret walked into the center of the tent. "Welcome, bakers." Her voice was sweet and kind. She reminded Comet of her grandmother. "My name is Terry Strawberry, and I'm here to judge this honored tradition. I remember competing in it myself, when I was still in school."

Comet had never thought about this baking competition as a tradition—no one talked about it like they talked about the hoofball match. There wasn't a case of trophies in the library or anything. Comet wondered how many students in the history of the school had entered, and if any of them had made the same mistakes she had.

"As you know, today you will be making a cake that best represents your school. I am looking forward to seeing what you've developed. You have one hour. Ready, set, bake!"

Comet stared at her workstation. She was reminded of

something Twilight had once told her, how a blank canvas was always the scariest. She looked at her friends and smiled. She knew just what to do. She had a plan, even if it was a last-minute one.

Soon the smells of the tent pulled her into her baking zone, and it felt like she was back in Stella and Celest's kitchen before all the baking competition and hoofball match business had begun. Back when she would stop by

just to see what they were cooking and if they would let her help. As if on cue, Stella yelled, "You can do it, Comet!"

"Shh, she's in the zone!" Celest said, trying to quiet Stella down.

Comet got to work, mixing the different doughs and frostings with her hooves. She tasted her cake mixtures and added more sugar here, and more butter there.

Time raced by, but she managed to get her cake layers into the oven in time. She was just finishing her decorations when she heard Terry Strawberry say, "Step away from your tables, bakers. Time is up."

Comet took a deep breath and looked at her cake, happy with knowing that she'd done her best.

11

The Flavors of
Unicorn University

"I made a crystalized sugar cake," the Glitterhorn baker explained as he presented his creation. "I chose this because I wanted it to glitter in the sunshine, just like Glitterhorn College!"

Comet thought the only word to describe his creation was "spectacular." The cake sparkled as if it were covered in diamonds.

Terry Strawberry sliced into the cake, cutting into the big letter *G* he had made out of powdered sugar in the center. "It certainly glitters, and is very sweet. Well done, Nova."

Comet's heart beat inside her chest. She wondered if she had made the wrong choice. *No turning back now.*

Comet looked down at her cake. She had draped over it the purple bandanna Flash had given her at the start of the game.

"I covered the cake in this bandanna because it represents the Unicorn University hoofball team, which our whole school is proud of. I wanted the bandanna to be the first thing people see because the team is often front and center at school."

Using her teeth, Comet pulled off the bandanna to reveal a tall cake covered with green frosting. On the top were the tiny sculptures Twilight and the art club had made. There

were a few little red barns, and there was a miniature version of the Crystal Library. The art club had even managed to create tiny trees.

"The outside of the cake is our campus, a beautiful place that all of us at Unicorn U have come to call home. I know we all think it's as magical as a rainbow. Miss Strawberry, would you mind slicing into the cake?"

"Of course not," she replied, her eyes sparkling behind her glasses. She sliced to reveal many different layers all stacked up on top of one another. The inside looked just like a rainbow.

"I layered lots of different flavors inside the cake. There's an apple-cider layer, an orange-and-cinnamon layer, and a candied-apple layer. Because Unicorn U has so many talented students. There's the baking club and dance club, the Sparklers and the science club. We're all different in our own ways, but together we make Unicorn University."

Terry Strawberry took a bite and chewed. It seemed to

Comet that she took way more time on this one that she had on Nova's. *Is that a good sign or a bad sign?* Comet worried.

"This is delicious, Comet. I especially like the orange-and-cinnamon layer. You both made wonderful desserts, and it's hard for me to declare a winner today in this tent. But I have been swayed by your creativity and heart, Comet. This cake has more personality than most. Congratulations. You have won the baking competition for Unicorn University!"

A big chorus of cheers surprised Comet, and she looked over to see the whole hoofball team standing at the sides of the tent. Comet could see that Flash was with the hoofball trophy. And there was Sapphire, cheering more loudly than anyone else.

12

As Sparkly As a Sugar Doughnut

"R eady, Comet?" Sapphire asked from outside her stall. It was the morning after the big day with Glitterhorn.

"As ready as I'll ever be," Comet said, her hoofball cape slung over her shoulder.

Sapphire and Comet walked toward the hoofball field. Comet was going to return her uniform to Coach. She was going to need to focus on baking, with the Five Kingdoms Bakeoff coming up. The two friends walked quietly, neither knowing quite what to say.

"Comet—"

"Sapphire—"

The two started laughing. By talking at the same time, they had somehow broken the spell that had kept them silent.

"Me first," Comet said. "I should have told you the truth. I know that now."

Sapphire shook her head. "I wasn't listening. I should've known something was up. It's just, I thought I wouldn't be able to play without you. I thought Coach only wanted me because I was paired up with you."

Comet nudged her friend gently with her flank. "I know how doubting yourself feels. Let's agree to never keep things from each other again."

That was a promise Comet knew she could keep.

As simple as that, the two unicorns were okay once more. Comet felt as sparkly as a sugar doughnut.

When Comet arrived at the Friendly Fields, she was surprised to see not only Coach but the whole hoofball team gathered together, and even Shamrock and Twilight stood off to the side.

Comet looked at Sapphire with surprise. "What's going on?"

Sapphire shook her head. "I have no clue."

Comet looked over to Shamrock and Twilight, but they shrugged, clearly also confused.

Just then the whole team jumped up and yelled, "Surprise!" They had strung up a banner that said, GO, BAKERS, GO!

Flash came to the front of the group and held out four aprons. She called Shamrock and Twilight over and draped an apron over each of the four friends' necks, as if the aprons were special garlands at the end of a winning game. "We know you're not on the hoofball team anymore, Comet, but we wanted you to know we are still cheering for you and your team of bakers!"

Comet felt so happy that her hooves floated right off the grass. For the first time ever, she didn't know what to say. Until finally she managed, "Go, Unicorn University!"

READ ON FOR A PEEK AT

Twilight's Grand Finale

Twilight looked down at her painter's smock and snorted in surprise. She was totally covered in paint! Her deep black coat was speckled with a rainbow of colors, and her hooficure was covered by blue and pink splotches. *Actually*, she thought, *this is a cool idea for a painting.* She imagined a big canvas filled with splattered colors.

But Twilight's dreams of future art projects were put on pause when a bright orange unicorn came running up to her. A giant cluster of colorful balloons bobbed behind them, and

Twilight noticed the strings were tied to the unicorn's horn.

"Hi, Sunny," Twilight said. "So cool—it looks like you're pulling a rainbow behind you."

Sunny stopped to catch their breath. "Thanks!" they said, still panting from the run over. "Where"—*huff*—"do you"—*huff*—"want them?"

Twilight bit her lip and tried to remember which booth needed balloons. She had been juggling so many tasks that she was losing track of things! Being in charge of all the decorations for the Unicorn University Annual Carnival meant that Twilight was responsible for everything from balloon decisions to booth painting to fireworks!

Unicorns from all over Sunshine Springs, and even some who lived in other parts of the five kingdoms, were traveling to Unicorn University for the celebration. Parents and siblings of current students would arrive tomorrow to visit with students and see the campus. Every year, the first years planned and set up the events of the carnival, meaning it was Twilight's class's turn. They had spent weeks thinking up game ideas, snacks, and, most exciting of all, a big surprise to end the night. It was tradition, and Twilight wanted this carnival to be one to remember.

"At the welcome booth!" Twilight finally remembered. That's where the balloons needed to go! "I can bring them over, Sunny. Why don't you take a snack break? The baking club made special apple cakes for everyone."

Sunny smiled wide. "You're the best, Twilight." They bent down their horn so Twilight could take the balloons, and then they jogged off in search of sweets.

When the art club had first asked Twilight to be in charge of decorations, she had thought they'd made a mistake. If someone had told her on her very first day at Unicorn University that she would be telling any other unicorn what to do, she would have whinnied in their face. But when she thought about the carnival, her big imagination took over and she couldn't help but think of all the ways to make things look beautiful. It had been her idea to have different clubs decorate their booths with materials they loved most, and the result was perfect. Twilight looked around at the booths around her. The garden club had decorated their booth with flowers; the science club had made a bubble machine that was burping up big, soapy bubbles; and the baking club had hung doughnuts and cookies at their booth.

Over at the baking booth, where Sunny was happily munching on apple cake, Twilight noticed that Comet, one of her best friends, was using her flying ability to frost the top of a giant cake with her horn. Twilight chuckled. Comet looked so serious, but she was totally covered in frosting! It made for a silly sight.

The balloons above Twilight's head bopped together as the wind whipped up, reminding her to get moving. As she walked toward the blue-and-white-striped welcome tent, the springtime smell of fresh flowers and sunshine wafted through the air, and the green grass under her hooves squished a little from the morning rain. Feeling lighter than air, Twilight skipped the rest of the way.

As she tied the balloons to one of the welcome tent's

poles, she heard a very familiar voice. And it did *not* sound very happy.

"One at a time! One at time!" a mint-colored unicorn yelled to a crowd of first years. It was Twilight's other good friend Shamrock, and she could see that his glasses were crooked and his mane was a mess. Twilight knew that the more rumpled Shamrock looked, the more ruffled he felt. *Uh-oh*, Twilight thought, *something must be wrong*. After finishing off her knot, Twilight headed over to help figure out the problem.

EBOOK EDITIONS ALSO AVAILABLE
From Aladdin
simonandschuster.com/kids

Mermaid Tales

Join Shelly and her mermaid friends in all of
their exciting adventures under the sea!

#1 TROUBLE AT TRIDENT ACADEMY

#2 BATTLE OF THE BEST FRIENDS

#3 A WHALE OF A TALE

#4 DANGER IN THE DEEP BLUE SEA

#5 THE LOST PRINCESS

#6 THE SECRET SEAHORSE

#7 DREAM OF THE BLUE TURTLE

#8 TREASURE IN TRIDENT CITY

#9 A ROYAL TEA

MermaidTalesBooks.com

Looking for another great book?
Find it
IN THE MIDDLE.

Fun, fantastic books for kids
in the in-be**TWEEN** age.

IntheMiddleBooks.com

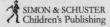

READ & LEARN

with *simon kids*

A one-stop shop where you can **find downloadable resources, watch interactive author videos, browse books by reading level, and more!**

Visit us at
SimonandSchusterPublishing.com/ReadandLearn/

And follow us @SimonKids

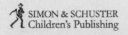

SIMON & SCHUSTER
Children's Publishing